www.mascotbooks.com

For more information, please contact:
Mascot Books
560 Herndon Parkway #120
Herndon, VA 20170
info@mascotbooks.com

CPSIA Code: PRW0514A
ISBN-13: 9781620867853

Printed in the United States

Hello, Clark!

Introducing the
Chicago Cubs New Mascot

Naren Aryal

Illustrated by Danny Moore

In 1916, the *Chicago Cubs* introduced their first-ever mascot.
His name was Joa and he was a black bear.

Joa loved everything about the *Cubs* and was so proud to be a part of their organization.

Joa later retired to the Lincoln Park Zoo where he spent
many days sharing tales with the animals in his den.

Clark™, one of Joa's great-grandcubs, loved listening to the stories. His favorite stories were about Joa's time as the *Cubs* mascot.

Clark™ loved the *Cubs*. Throughout the day, he would think about the *Cubs*, wondering what it would be like to play on the team.

At night, he would dream about hitting the game-winning homerun in the bottom of the ninth.

One afternoon, *Clark*™ heard loud noises coming from down the street. He wasn't quite sure what it was so, being a curious bear, he followed it. The loud noises led him to...

...*Wrigley Field*!

Clark™ was hearing the cheering fans!

Clark™ wanted to see what was going on so he climbed up the side of *Wrigley Field* and peered over the edge. The *Cubs* had beaten their rivals and were raising the 'W' flag.

It was a wonderful sight to see. *Clark*™ couldn't help but climb into the stands, clapping and cheering along with the rest of the fans.

It didn't take long for people to notice *Clark*™. Fans and players were pointing and talking about him, wondering who he was and what he was doing there.

Clark™ just waved to everyone and said, "Hi! I'm *Clark*™," and continued cheering on his *Cubs*.

After the game, one of the team representatives approached
Clark™. "We love to see such enthusiasm in our fans, *Clark*™.
How would you like to be the *Cubs* official mascot?"

Clark™ couldn't believe it! His dream was coming true!
"I would like that very much," he said graciously.

On his first day as the official mascot,
Clark™ couldn't get out of bed fast enough.

After brushing his teeth, combing his fur, and dressing
in his *Cubs* gear, he was on his way.

As *Clark*™ approached *Wrigley Field*, he could see *Cubs* fans everywhere he looked. A few of them seemed to remember him from the last game.

"Hello, *Clark*™!" they shouted and waved at him.

"Hello! Go *Cubs*!" he shouted, waving back.

"Play ball!" yelled the umpire. The *Cubs* pitcher delivered
a fastball to start the game. Strike one!

Clark™ cheered loudly. The game was off to a good start.

When it was time for the seventh inning stretch, *Clark*™ led the
crowd as everyone sang "Take Me Out to the Ballgame".

Young *Cubs* fans danced on the dugout with *Clark*™.
They helped him start a "Let's Go *Cubs*!" chant.

The *Cubs* won the game! Once the players left the field, *Clark*™ found more young *Cubs* fans to join him in running the bases.

Everyone had fun pretending they were a part of the *Cubs* team!

It was a fun day at *Wrigley Field*, but *Clark*™ sure was tired. As he left the field, he waved goodbye to all his new friends, excited to see them again soon.

But for now, it was time to go home.

Goodnight, *Clark*™!